Marco Moonlight

Clyde Robert Bulla

MARCO MOONLIGHT

ILLUSTRATED BY

Julia Noonan

A YEARLING BOOK

To David and Bill White

Published by
Dell Publishing Co., Inc.
1 Dag Hammarskjold Plaza
New York, New York 10017

Yearling ® TM 913705, Dell Publishing Co., Inc.

ISBN: 0-440-45848-X

Reprinted by arrangement with Harper & Row, Publishers,
Inc., on behalf of.Thomas Y. Crowell Co.
Printed in the United States of America
First Yearling printing—January 1979

CW

Contents

CHAPTER ONE

Dorn Hall

O N THAT STILL, spring morning—
the morning of his birthday—
Marco had the dream again. He
was awake when it came to him. He
knew he was awake because he could
see the oak posts at the foot of his bed.
He could feel the cool air coming in
through the window. He could hear a
bird singing.

He closed his eyes, trying to keep the
dream a little longer, but it was quickly
gone.

He sat up. On a chair by the bed was
his new suit. He had hung it there the
night before so he would remember to

wear it on his birthday. Today he was thirteen.

He put on the suit and ran downstairs.

In the sunny breakfast room he found Grandmother and Grandfather. They were at the table, drinking coffee. A blazing fire had been built to warm their old bones.

Before he could tell them about the dream, they said together, "Happy birthday, Marco!"

He kissed Grandmother and shook Grandfather's hand.

"A fine day for your birthday," said Grandfather.

"A fine day for the party," said Grandmother.

She rang for breakfast.

Cook must have been waiting outside. She came running in with a tray of porridge and brown sugar and cream and cinnamon buns and orange marma-

lade. She bobbed her head three times and said, "Happy birthday, Master Marco."

"Thank you, Mary," he said.

When she was gone, he said, "I had the dream again."

"The dream?" said Grandmother. "Oh, yes."

"But I was awake," he said. "All the time I was awake."

"That's not so strange," said Grandmother. "We all have daydreams."

"What do you mean, you had the dream?" asked Grandfather. "What dream is that?"

"You know," said Grandmother. "The one he always has."

"I don't remember," said Grandfather.

"I dreamed I was a baby," Marco told him. "I was playing with another baby. He was my brother. We had some string, and we were pulling it back and forth between us. Then someone took my brother away, and I cried."

Grandfather blinked his eyes. "That's odd."

"And my mother was there." Marco asked, "Do you think it was more than a dream? Do you think it's something I remember?"

"What did your mother look like in the dream?" asked Grandmother.

"Like the big picture in the library," answered Marco.

"Ah, you see," said Grandmother. "It was really her picture you were dreaming about. You couldn't remember *her*. You couldn't remember anything before we brought you to Dorn Hall. You were too young."

Marco said suddenly, "Tell me about my mother. Tell me the story."

"You've heard it a hundred times," she said. "And it's not a story I *like* telling."

"I didn't know you minded," said Marco.

"Well, I do. But I'll tell it once more, because you asked me. Because it's your birthday."

She told the story.

"Your mother was our little girl— the only one we had. Her name was Katharine. We called her Kate. She grew up here at Dorn Hall, and she was a happy child. She liked to ride. She liked to walk to the seashore.

"When she was grown she met a young man named Stephen Moonlight. He looked like a prince, but he was the wrong man for her. He was poor—"

"It isn't wrong to be poor," said Marco.

"But he pretended to be rich," said Grandmother. "He never told the truth about himself. We tried to tell her, but she wouldn't listen."

Grandmother went on with the story. Kate ran away and married Stephen Moonlight. For more than three years they heard nothing of her. Then a letter came from a woman in the north country. Grandmother still had the letter. She had shown it to Marco, and he knew it by heart:

. . . Your daughter came to my inn a week ago. She is ill, and I am caring for her and her child. The child's name is Marco, and he will be two years old on May Day. Your daughter and her husband have parted. She does not know what has become of him. She is sorry she went against your wishes, and she begs you to come to her. . . .

Grandfather and Grandmother went to the north country. They found the inn and the woman who had written the letter.

"Your mother was dead," Grandfather told Marco. "We brought you back to Dorn Hall."

Marco asked, "Where was my brother?"

Grandmother sighed. "There was no brother."

"But I remember him," said Marco.

"You never had a brother," said Grandmother. "It was one of your dreams."

Marco sat looking into the fire.

"You mustn't look so sad," said Grandfather.

"You'll smile when you see what Cook made for your party," said Grandmother.

"I don't want a party," said Marco.

"Oh, Marco!" cried Grandmother. "You don't mean that!"

At once he was sorry and ashamed. Grandmother and Grandfather were so kind to him. They always had been.

"No, I don't mean it," he said. He smiled, and they smiled back and wished him a happy birthday all over again.

CHAPTER TWO

The Man in the Village

THE PARTY was to be outdoors. Old Varley, the gardener, had worked all morning getting the garden ready. He had picked every dead leaf off the rose bushes. He had raked the paths. He had set a circle of chairs under the elm tree.

Thirty-one boys and girls had been asked to the party. They were the sons and daughters of the farmers who worked on Grandfather's land.

"It makes a happy time for them," Grandmother said to Marco. "Besides, it lets them know you're not proud."

Marco was at the gate to meet them.

Some were small. A few were near his own age. Some were almost grown.

Each one said, "Happy birthday, Master Marco," and gave him a gift. There were handkerchiefs and scarfs. There were marbles and beanbags. There was a wooden whistle.

The boys and girls sat in the shade. Most of them looked uncomfortable in their good clothes. They talked in whispers until the games began.

They played tag and hide-and-go-seek. They ran carefully so as not to spoil the grass. With the walls of Dorn Hall looking down on them, they didn't laugh or shout. It would have been like laughing or shouting in church.

Grandmother and Grandfather came out. Grandmother was in wine-colored satin, and Grandfather wore a black suit.

They said, "Welcome—welcome, one and all."

Grandmother spoke to everyone. "So this is Jenny. How pretty you look! . . . And this is Joseph. What a help you must be to your father."

Grandfather asked, "Have you had the races? We came to see the races."

The youngest children went first. They ran across the garden and back in a long, crooked line.

Marco ran with the older ones. Joseph and Charley were tall farmboys, older and bigger than he was. At the start they left him far behind, but at the finish he was ahead.

Grandfather stood up and clapped his hands. "Well done, boy!" he called out.

Marco's face was hot. He said half angrily to Joseph and Charley, "You had me beat. You know you did. Why did you let me win?"

"No, no, Master Marco," said Charley.

"We ran our best," said Joseph. "You won it fair."

But it wasn't true. They had let him win because he was Master Marco—because their fathers worked for his grandfather. It was always this way, and he hated it!

Cook brought out the surprise. It was a birthday cake so big and so pink that the farm children went "Ah-h!" when they saw it. Marco blew out the candles and cut the first piece. Everyone sat in a circle and ate cake and drank punch.

When the birthday cake was gone, there were more cakes—tiny round ones with red sugar on top. One little girl ate four, then cried with the stomachache. Some of the smaller children cried, too, because they were tired and away from home.

The party broke up. Boys and girls

left, until only a few of the older ones were there.

Marco felt reckless. Up to now, the afternoon had been dull. Surely he had a right to a little fun on his own birthday.

He called Tim, the stableboy. "Hitch Jip to the cart."

"You want the pony and cart?" asked Grandfather.

"Where are you going?" asked Grandmother.

"To the village and back," said Marco.

"Are you sure that's what you want to do?" asked Grandfather.

"It's his birthday," Grandmother said, "and he's a good driver."

Tim brought up the shaggy black pony hitched to the cart.

"Come on," said Marco. "We're going for a ride."

Charley was still there, and two of

the girls, Jenny and Eva. They got into the cart. Marco got in after them. "Hi, Jip!" he shouted, and they were off.

It was a mile to the village. They passed a wagon and two carriages on the way. They stopped on top of a hill to rest the pony.

"Look, there's the sea," said Jenny.

"Let's watch for ships," said Eva.

They watched until they saw a white sail a long way off. Then they went on to the village.

The square was quiet. They drove past the mill and the tavern and came to Miss Dolly's Sweet Shop.

"Who wants a sweet?" asked Marco.

"Not I." Charley rolled his eyes and rubbed his stomach. "Not after the birthday cake!"

Jenny was looking at the window of the sweet shop. "See the lovely bunch of grapes."

"It can't be," said Charley. "There won't be grapes till fall."

"There they are, all the same," said Jenny.

"They can't be real," said Charley.

"Let's go see." Marco jumped out and tied the pony to a post. They went up to the shop and looked through the window.

"I told you," said Charley.

"It's candy!" said Jenny.

"The leaves, too!" said Eva. "Purple candy for the grapes, green candy for the—"

She stopped. A man had come out of the tavern. He was there beside them, and his shadow lay over them all. He made a strange, choking sound in his throat.

"*You—!*" he said.

His eyes were on Marco.

Marco looked back at him. The man wore a short jacket and a black leather cap. He had a broad face and a snub nose. His neck was thick and short. His hair grew long—curly, black hair with bits of gray in it. Marco had never seen him before.

The man reached out, as if he meant to seize Marco or strike him. His eyes were staring.

Marco did not move. "What do you want?" he asked.

All the strength seemed to go out of the man. He leaned against the door of the shop.

Charley spoke in a low voice. "Let's go."

The girls got into the cart. Charley and Marco got in after them. They drove away.

"Who was he?" Marco asked the others.

None of them knew.

"The way he looked at you—!" said Jenny. "Like he was . . . *surprised.*"

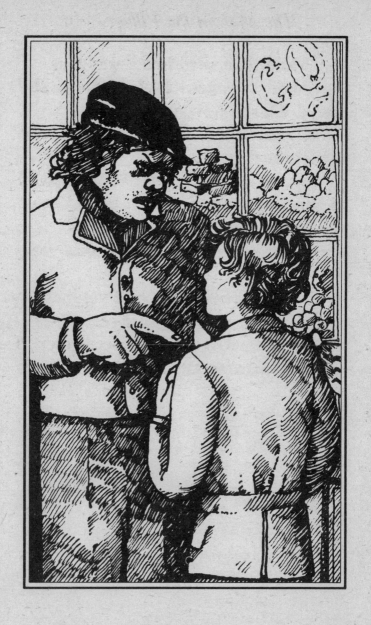

"More than surprised," said Eva.

Charley looked back. "He's still there. Maybe he's sick."

Marco pulled the pony to a walk. "We'd better go see."

"If you please, Master Marco, I don't want to go back there," said Jenny.

"I don't either, if you please," said Eva.

Both girls were pale, and there was a scared look on Charley's face.

Marco drove on. They were quiet all the way back to Dorn Hall.

CHAPTER THREE

Old Varley

A FEW DAYS after the birthday party, Grandfather had a talk with Marco. He talked about his farms and how they were run.

"Someday you will be master here," he said. "You're old enough now to think about it and what it will mean to you."

Marco didn't want to think about it. He tried to put it out of his mind, but Grandfather's words kept coming back.

That night he couldn't sleep. He went down into the garden, sat under the elm tree, and looked up at the stars.

He had been there only a little while when he heard footsteps. Someone

came around the corner of the house—
a man in a hat and a long cloak. The
man was walking softly.

Marco held his breath. Then he
smiled to himself. The man was Varley.

Almost every night the old gardener
slipped off to the village.

"So he likes to sit with his friends in
the tavern," said Grandmother. "So he
likes his pint of ale. I'll not scold him
for that."

"Nor I," said Grandfather, "but pretend you don't know. It's his pleasure
to think he has a secret from us.
There's no harm as long as he does his
work the next day."

Marco was hidden in the shadows.
Varley walked past without seeing him.
The gate opened and closed, and he was
gone.

Marco sat there until the air grew
chill. Then he went back inside.

In the morning he met Cook on the stairs. She looked worried.

"Master Marco, have you seen Varley?" she asked.

He shook his head. "Not today."

"I tapped on his door," she said, "but he's never come out to breakfast. Do you think somebody had better go see—?"

Marco went around to the back of Dorn Hall where the servants slept. He knocked at Varley's door. There was no answer.

He opened the door and went into the tiny room. Varley was not there. His work shoes were under the bed. His good shoes were gone. He looked at the rack on the wall where Varley hung his clothes. His hat and cloak were not there.

Marco found Cook and told her, "Varley isn't in his room."

"He went out last night," she said. "I heard him."

"I know," said Marco, "and I don't think he ever came home."

"Most likely he had a drop too many and went to sleep by the road."

"He's never done that," said Marco.

"There's always a first time," she said.

Marco took the pony and cart and drove off toward the village. He looked along the road. He saw no sign of Varley.

In the village he stopped at the tavern. He spoke to Bob, the young man behind the bar. "Was Varley here last night?"

"Varley?" The young man scratched his head. "I really couldn't say."

"It's all right to tell me," said Marco. "We know he comes here. I'm asking because he didn't come home last night."

"Bless my soul!" said Bob. "I remember now. He *was* here. He stayed an hour. Maybe two. He was walking as straight as you please when he left here."

A man had come up behind Marco. He spoke in a strong, deep voice. "Pardon me. Perhaps I can help."

It was a voice Marco had hardly heard before, yet somehow he knew it. He turned. The man who stood there was the stranger he had met outside the sweet shop.

"I see you remember me," said the man.

"I do," said Marco.

"You may not remember me kindly." The man was smiling. "My name is Flint, and I'd like a word with you."

"I've no time," said Marco. "I'm looking for—"

"I know, I know," the man broke in, "but let me say this. The day we met I wasn't quite myself. I'd just taken a room here at the tavern, and I'd sent a boy out for tobacco. When he didn't come back, I was angry. I thought, the next time I see him, I'll shake him up. When I saw you on the street, I thought you were that boy. He was your size. Then I saw your face and I knew I was mistaken."

The words were well spoken, yet there was something false about them.

"Before I could explain, you were gone," the man went on. "I've been wanting a chance to—"

"It's no matter," said Marco. "I must go now to find my grandfather's gardener—"

"Whose name is Varley," said Flint.

Marco asked quickly, "Do you know him?"

"Yes. We talked here last night."

"Was he well?" asked Marco.

"Quite well," said Flint. "Why?"

"He hasn't come home, and I was afraid—"

"He hasn't come home? I was with him when he left here. I saw him walk off down the road."

"Then he must be somewhere between here and Dorn Hall," said Marco, "but I've looked all along the road."

"Perhaps you should look again. Perhaps you should ask along the way. Have you done this?"

"No," said Marco.

"Come. I'll go with you."

They left the tavern. Marco drove away. Flint walked beside the cart.

"Ride if you like," said Marco.

"Your cart is a bit small for me. Besides, I like to stretch my legs." Flint said, as he walked along, "I'm anxious about the old man. The last two or three nights we've talked in the tavern. We've come to be friends."

They crossed the bridge.

"Did you look under here?" asked Flint.

"No," said Marco.

Flint looked under the bridge. "No one there."

They went on. They came to a thicket of trees beside the road.

"Did you look in here?" asked Flint.

"No," answered Marco.

Flint disappeared among the trees. In a few minutes he was back. His face was grave.

"Come," he said.

Marco tied the pony to a bush. He went with Flint into the thicket. He gave a start. Old Varley was there, lying on his back in the tall grass. His

hat was beside him. His cloak was open. One arm was twisted beneath him.

Flint knelt beside the old man. He put a hand over his heart. "He's alive."

Marco knelt, too. He tried to straighten Varley's arm. The old man gave a moan of pain.

"He's been beaten," said Flint. "Look at these marks on his head. Someone must have dragged him off the road and robbed him."

"We've no robbers here!" said Marco.

"Ah, lad, you never know." Flint lifted Varley's head and shoulders. "Help me here. Take his feet. That's it."

They carried him to the cart and lifted him in.

"There. Take him along," said Flint. "I'll run back to the village for a doctor."

"Thank you for your help," said Marco.

At first he had not trusted the stranger. Now he began to feel a liking for the man.

CHAPTER FOUR

Flint

THE DOCTOR came out on horse-back. Varley was in his bed, able to talk.

Marco stood by while the doctor dressed Varley's wounds. The old man tried to tell them what had happened.

"I was coming home, and I could hear a man walking behind me, and I said, 'Who is it?' and he didn't say anything, so I knew he was no friend. I went into the trees and waited for him to go by, but he came into the trees, too. I tried to get away, but he caught hold of me and pulled me around. That was the last I knew."

"What did he look like?" asked Marco.

"I couldn't see. It was dark in there."

The old man had been struck twice on the head. There were cuts about his chest, and his left arm was broken.

"He's black and blue all over," said the doctor. "I'd say he'd been beaten with a club."

"Who would do this to him!" said Marco. "Wasn't it enough to take his money?"

"How much did he have?" asked the doctor.

"Seven pennies," said Varley, and he gave a cackling laugh. "Seven pennies is all he got for his trouble!"

"Maybe that's why Varley was beaten," the doctor said to Marco. "Maybe the robber was angry because he'd got so little."

Flint came to the door. He had

walked out from the village. "How is he?" he asked.

"His arm is the worst," said the doctor. "It's a bad break."

"Who's there?" Varley tried to sit up. "Is it my friend?"

Flint went to the bed. "I'm the one who found you. How are you, man?"

"Broken," answered Varley. "I feel all broken up inside."

"You'll feel better." Flint patted the old man's shoulder. "I'll leave you now. You need your rest. But I'll be back to see how you're getting on."

Marco walked with him to the front gate. Grandfather was in the garden.

"This is Flint," said Marco.

"The one who found Varley and sent the doctor out? We thank you," said Grandfather.

Flint bowed. "Always glad to help, sir. I look on the old man as a friend.

We had some good talks at the tavern.
He was proud of the garden here and
wanted me to see it."

"Look about if you like," said
Grandfather.

"Thank you. I had a look on the way
in. It's a big garden to care for."

"That it is," said Grandfather.
"We'll be missing our gardener."

"I can see that," said Flint. "Good
day, sir," and he was gone.

Grandfather said, "He's a kind man,
I'm sure. Where does he come from?"

"He didn't say," answered Marco.

Flint was back the next morning.
After he had sat for half an hour with
Varley, he asked Marco, "May I have a
word with the master of the house?"

Marco took him into the library,
where Grandfather was reading.

Flint stopped in the doorway. He was
looking at the large painting on the

wall. It was a picture of Marco's
mother, smiling and beautiful, with the
wind blowing her long, brown hair.

"Good morning," said Grandfather.

"Good morning." Flint bowed.
"There's something I'd like to ask, sir.
While Varley is mending, how would it
be if I took on a bit of his work?"

Grandfather looked surprised. "Are
you a gardener?"

"Yes and no, sir. You might say I
have a feeling for the soil. Yesterday I
saw a thing or two that needed doing,
and I thought—"

"Certainly, certainly," said Grandfather. "Shall we talk about pay?"

"Thank you, sir," said Flint, "but
this is for Varley."

Afterward Marco sat with Grandfather. Through the window they
watched Flint in the garden. He
weeded a bed of herbs. He loosened the
earth around the rose bushes. When he

had finished, he gathered up the tools and took them back to the shed.

"He does seem to know about gardening," said Marco.

"That he does," said Grandfather, "and a good many other things, I'd guess."

Every day for a week Flint came to see Varley. Each time he worked an hour or two in the garden.

One afternoon Grandmother, Grandfather, and Marco were having tea out under the elm. Flint finished his work and came over to speak to them.

"I've had a talk with Varley," he said. "He tells me he'll be leaving soon."

"Yes, poor fellow," said Grandfather. "He'll never be strong enough to work again. His daughter is coming to take him home with her."

"So he told me," said Flint. "Have you another gardener in mind?"

"Perhaps the son of one of my farmers," said Grandfather.

"Would you think of me for the place?" asked Flint.

"You?"

"Why not, sir?" asked Flint.

Grandfather said, "I thought you might be above working as a gardener."

"Not at all. It's pleasant at Dorn Hall. Of course, you know little about me."

"I know enough, I should think."

"That's kind of you, but perhaps you should know more. I was born on a farm beyond Moresby. I ran away to sea when I was a boy. When I came back, I found myself alone in the world. I worked at farming and printing. I was a carpenter. I came to the village here in search of a man who owed me money. I never found him, but I found kindness, so I stayed."

"Then let us hope you've found a home here," said Grandfather. "Come to work any day you like."

CHAPTER FIVE

The House on the Beach

VARLEY'S DAUGHTER came the next day. The old man rode off with her in her wagon. Marco and Grandmother and Grandfather were at the gate to wave good-by. Flint and the other servants were there, too, waving as the wagon disappeared down the road.

Grandmother and Grandfather walked slowly into the garden. Marco went with them.

Grandmother said, as they sat in the shade, "Varley planted these rose bushes. He was a part of Dorn Hall. Now we'll never see him here again."

"This is a sad day," said Grandfather.

"I beg your pardon . . ." said a voice.

They looked up. Flint was there, cap in hand. "I wanted to ask you—" he began.

"About your room?" asked Grandfather. "You're free to move in."

Flint was quiet. His gray eyes seemed to look far away.

"There's something on your mind," said Grandfather. "Speak up."

Flint said, "When I'm new in a place, I explore. It's a thing I always do. When I first came to the village, I explored the country here. I went as far as the sea where the cliffs are."

"Smugglers' Cliffs," said Grandfather. "That's what we call them."

"There's a break in the cliffs where you can walk down to a beach," said

Flint. "There are houses on the beach. I'm told they belong to you."

Grandfather nodded. "There are three houses, built in my father's time. He thought friends might like to live there in the summer, but they never did. There was always something gloomy, something *gray* about the beach that no one liked. Later some of the coal miners lived there until the mines closed. The houses have stood empty for years."

"Would you give me leave to live in one of them?" asked Flint.

Grandfather stared at him. "But— you'd be miles from your work."

"Not many miles," said Flint, "and I'm a good walker."

Marco told him, "I was down there last winter. Not one of those houses is fit to live in."

"There's one that would do, I

think," said Flint. "It needs a bit of work, and that I could do myself."

Grandfather frowned. "I don't understand you. Why should you live in such a far and lonely place when there's a room for you here?"

"It's a fine room, sir," said Flint, "only . . ."

"Only what?"

"It's a little small. You see," Flint went on quickly, "here and there about the country I have books stored away. One day I'd like to bring them all together. And Varley's old room wouldn't hold the half of them."

"What kind of books are these?" asked Grandfather.

"Just books, sir. Books for reading."

Grandmother touched Grandfather's arm. "Like the ones in your library. You're fond of them. You know you are. Why shouldn't this man be fond of his?"

"No reason. No reason at all. But when a man works for me, I want him to have a good roof over his head."

"Give me leave to try one of the houses," said Flint. "If it wants a good roof, I'll put one on."

"Do as you think best," said Grandfather. "Have another look at the houses. You may change your mind."

"Thank you, sir. If I may, I'll walk over today." Flint looked at Marco. "Perhaps the young gentleman would keep me company."

Flint and Marco walked toward the sea. Near Smugglers' Cliffs there were no more farms, and the road ended. They crossed a stony field and came to the break in the cliffs.

The way down through the break was steep and narrow. They came out on the short strip of beach where the houses were.

Two of the houses were side by side at one end of the beach. The third house stood alone at the other end. All were small, stone cottages. The two that stood together were falling to pieces. The one that stood alone had four good walls, but half the roof was gone.

The door of the lone house was open. They went inside and walked through the two rooms. There were sticks and stones on the floor. Sand had drifted in.

Flint stepped on an iron ring. It was fastened to a trapdoor in the floor. He lifted the door and looked down a stone stairway.

"There's a cellar underneath," Marco said. "It's where people went when there was a storm. Most houses here have storm cellars."

"Ah, yes." Flint let the door fall shut.

The damp smell of the cellar had come up into the room. Marco held his breath until he could get outside. Flint came out, too.

"You can see why nobody wants to live here," said Marco.

"Why?" asked Flint.

"It's so gloomy. The beach is so small and shut-in. The cliffs keep out the sun more than half the day, and there's always a sad feeling. Don't you feel it?"

"I can't say I do. I keep thinking how the house is going to look with my books up on the walls."

"You really mean to live here?"

"Why shouldn't I, Master Marco?"

"The windows—"

"They can be mended."

"The roof—"

"That can be mended, too. I can take slate from the other two roofs." Flint was looking up at the cliffs. "What's this? A road?"

"Yes," answered Marco. "Some people say the smugglers used it a hundred years ago. Then the coal miners used it. It was a short cut to the mines."

"Who uses it now?"

"No one."

"Shall we explore it?"

"It might not be safe."

"I see. And once you're up there, it's a long way down." Flint was smiling. "The safe roads are best. Isn't that right, Master Marco? Come, let's go." And he led the way back through the break in the cliffs.

CHAPTER SIX

A Man Alone

FLINT TOLD Grandfather, "The house *is* a long way from my work."

"Yes," said Grandfather. "It's much too far."

"But I'd like it to go to," said Flint. "Perhaps on Sundays and rainy days. And it would be a place for my books and papers."

"Of course," said Grandfather.

So Flint moved into Varley's old room. Every morning he was busy in the garden. Almost every afternoon Grandfather gave him time to work on the house by the sea.

One day Marco went with Flint to

the beach. He said, when he saw the house, "It looks—" He stopped himself. He had almost said, "It looks like a prison!"

There were wooden bars at the windows. There was a heavy lock on the door.

"I want no one walking in while I'm away," said Flint.

"I don't think anyone would walk in. Anyway, people hardly ever come here." Marco asked, "Do you have your bookshelves yet?"

"No, but let me show you something." Flint took Marco down to the edge of the shore. "See what the tide brought in—all these good boards."

Marco looked at the gray-green boards that had been piled on the sand. "They must be from an old shipwreck."

"They'll make good bookshelves," said Flint. "Now if the sea would only

bring me a table and some chairs!" He
sat down on the pile of boards. He took
off his cap and ran his fingers through
his hair. "Do you think it strange," he
asked, "that I should want this place of
my own?"

"I? No," said Marco.

"There are some who think it
strange."

"Who?"

"Some of the servants at Dorn Hall.
Because I choose to read and study,
because I keep to myself, they say I'm
not one of them. And I'm not. I don't
deny it. I'm not one of them. And I'll
never be!" Color had come up into
Flint's cheeks. "Except for ill luck, I
might have been high in the world—as
high as you or anyone else. And someday—someday . . ." He stopped and
gave his head an odd little shake.
"Don't mind me. Sometimes I get
carried away by my own thoughts."

The sun had gone behind a bank of clouds. The air had turned cool.

"It *is* gloomy here," said Flint. "Shall we be off?"

They walked back to Dorn Hall.

"I thank you for your company," said Flint. "A man like me needs a friend. I hope you and I are friends, Master Marco."

Then he was gone, around the corner of the house to his room. Marco was thinking: *Were* they friends? Almost every day they were together. Flint told tales Marco liked to hear.

But sometimes the gardener's eyes were cold, his voice was hard. "A man with a secret"—that was what Cook called him. "A man alone," he called himself. Was there truly a secret? And why was he a man alone?

Were they friends, he and Flint? Marco could not be sure.

A few days later he woke early to the sound of voices below. He sat up in bed and looked out. Flint was crossing the driveway. He was dressed in clothes Marco had never seen before—high boots, a tan coat, and a black hat. He let himself out the front gate.

Marco put on his clothes and ran downstairs to the breakfast room. Grandfather and Grandmother were there.

"Where is Flint going?" he asked.

"To the village," said Grandfather. "He's off to hire a carriage and horses. He'll be away for a day or two."

"He wanted an early start," said Grandmother. "He said to tell you good-by."

"Why does he need a carriage?" asked Marco.

"He's going somewhere beyond Moresby, I think," said Grandfather.

"He wants to get some things he left there."

Cook brought Marco's breakfast. She put down the tray and marched out without a word.

"She's upset," said Grandmother. "She says she's worked every day for years. She says it isn't fair that Flint has so much free time."

"He did the weeding and watering before he left," said Grandfather. "If he wants to be away for a little while, I see no harm in it."

"Cook never liked him," Grandmother said. "She says he puts himself above the other servants."

"Jealous people," said Grandfather. "He's fond of his books, and he's been about the world. They're bound to be jealous."

"They'll get used to him, don't you think?" said Grandmother.

"They'd better," answered Grandfather. "He's the best gardener I ever
had, and I mean to keep him."

CHAPTER SEVEN

The Locked Door

FLINT WAS GONE for two days. On the morning of the third day he was back at work.

Marco talked with him in the garden.

"I heard you come in last night."

"Yes. It was late." Flint's face looked puffy, and he sounded tired. "I've been a long way."

"Did you bring your books?"

"My books? Oh, yes. Some of them."

"Where are they?"

"In the house on the beach."

"You mean you took them there last night?"

"I thought it best to take them while I had the carriage."

"But you couldn't drive the carriage all the way to the beach."

"No, Master Marco. I drove as near as I could. Then I carried the books the rest of the way."

"Why didn't you tell someone? You could have had help."

"It's all done. Don't you worry about it," said Flint. "I'm glad the books are here at last. Perhaps you'd like a look at them."

"What kind are they?"

"What kind do you like?"

"Books about other places," answered Marco. "Books with maps."

"Then you'll like what I brought," Flint told him. "If your grandfather will give me the time, I'll take you to see them tomorrow."

They set out early the next afternoon. The day was warm until they went down through the break in the cliffs. Near the sea the air was cool.

They stopped at the door of Flint's house. Flint rattled the key in the lock. "Sometimes it sticks," he said rather loudly. He opened the door and they went inside.

"You see I have furniture," said Flint.

The furniture was two empty wooden boxes. They looked water-stained, as if they had been brought up by the sea.

Marco turned toward the other room. "Are the books in here?"

"Let's not hurry. Sit down. We'll have a bit of a talk." Flint's voice had changed. It was mocking. He shut the door and locked it.

"You locked the door," said Marco.

"Did I? Are you sure?"

"Of course, I'm sure."

"Then," said Flint, "it must be true. You're a bright lad and not one to make mistakes."

Marco said, "Do you have any books for me to see? If you have, I'll look at them. If you haven't, I'll be going."

"Don't speak of going. Not so soon. Do you like games? Play this game with me. Pretend you're just Marco and I'm Master Flint. Now. What do you say?"

Flint's eyes were hard and bright. Marco felt a chill.

Then he was listening. Something had moved in the other room.

The door between the rooms was closed. It was made of rough boards nailed together. There were cracks between the boards. Through one of the cracks an eye was looking at him!

"There's someone—" he began.

Flint disappeared into the room. He closed the door after him.

Marco heard whispers that grew

louder. He heard Flint say, "I told you to stay quiet. I told you to wait until—"

There was another voice. "I've had enough of being quiet—in this hole two days and a night. I've got to come out sometime, and I'm coming out now!"

The door opened. A boy stood there —a slim boy with fair hair and blue eyes.

Marco stared into his face. It was like looking into a mirror. It was like looking at himself . . .

"Don't you know me?" asked the boy.

Marco shook his head.

"Have a guess," said the boy.

Marco tried to speak. No words would come.

"I'm your brother," said the boy. "I'm your very own twin brother!"

CHAPTER EIGHT

Down the Steps

I'm your brother . . . I'm your brother . . .

Over and over the words seemed to beat in Marco's ears. He *had* remembered. Long ago there *had* been that other boy, and now he was here!

"You're my brother," he said in a whisper. "Where—where have you been?"

"Out in the cold," said the boy in the doorway. "Out in the cold, while you lived like a king."

"Well said, Matt." Flint clapped the boy on the back. "You've told him. Have you kept your ears open? Have you caught his way of speaking?"

"I have. He talks like this." The boy spoke more clearly and put his voice a little higher. " 'My name is Marco Moonlight, and I'm master here.' "

"That's close enough," said Flint. "The old ones are so deaf they won't know the difference. Let's look at your hair . . . yes. Yours is longer."

He took a pair of scissors out of his pocket and snipped off some of the boy's hair.

"Matt—? Is your name Matt?" asked Marco. "If you were out in the cold, you didn't have to be. Why didn't you come to me? Why didn't—?"

"Sorry to end this tender scene," said Flint, "but there's no more time. Let's have your clothes."

Marco looked at him, trying to understand.

"Don't stand there like a stick," said Matt. He was pulling off his shirt.

"Give us your clothes. You're going to change with me."

Marco hardly heard the words. A thought had come to him, and there was something he had to know. He asked Flint, "Are you Stephen Moonlight? Are you my father?"

Flint's face turned darker. "No, I'm *not* your father. I'm nobody's father. And if you don't give me your clothes, I'll take them !"

Marco took off his clothes. Flint handed them over to Matt. Matt threw his clothes down in front of Marco, and Marco put them on. They were shabby and far from clean. The shoes were old and broken.

Matt was walking about in Marco's clothes. "I like this. Already I like it. And I'm going to like having my own bed and my own room and telling the servants what I want."

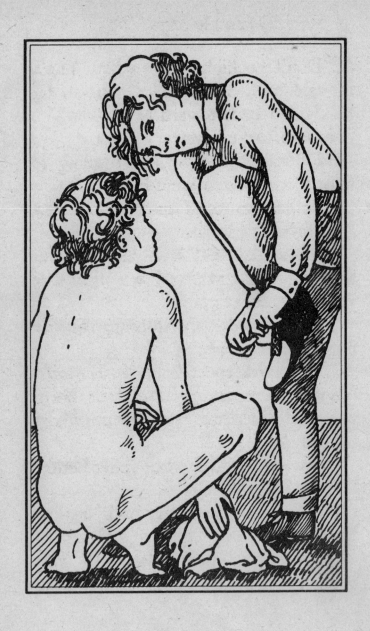

"Don't be high and mighty. You'll do as I say." Flint had a rope in his hands. He came toward Marco.

Marco backed away.

Flint said to Matt, "He's going to fight it. Give me a hand here."

"Forget the rope," said Matt.

"Forget it?"

"The cellar will hold him without the rope," said Matt. "I was all over it yesterday, and I know."

Flint seemed to be thinking. Slowly he put the rope aside.

"Why are you doing this?" cried Marco. "I've done nothing to harm you, and I'd *never* wish to harm my brother."

Flint had lifted the cellar door. "Down you go."

Marco stood with his back against the wall.

"Better go," said Matt. "If you don't, you'll get a helping hand. And a tumble down those steps could break your bones."

Marco looked down the stone steps.

"If you'd rather have the rope . . ." said Flint.

Marco went to the top of the stairs. The stones were damp. When he set foot on the top step, he slipped and half fell. Almost before he had reached the bottom, the door had dropped shut over his head.

CHAPTER NINE

The Dark Prison

THE OUTSIDE door closed, and the house was still.

In the darkness Marco stumbled up the cellar steps. He pushed at the trapdoor with his head and hands. He could not move it. He remembered now that he had heard a sound like a metal bolt sliding into place. The trapdoor was locked.

He went back down and slowly felt his way around the walls. They were of stone, and they were solid. The floor, too, was of stone.

He sat on the steps. The cellar was damp, as if water had seeped in.

This was his prison. His brother had helped put him here.

His brother . . .

He thought: I have a brother, a twin brother who looks like me. His name is Matt, and he was here. Now he is gone, dressed in my clothes, calling himself by my name. Why? What does it mean?

He began to feel ill. He put his head down on his knees.

After a long time he slept, a sleep that was half waking. He dreamed he was falling. When he woke, he was falling off the steps. He caught himself.

The stairs were a little less damp than the floor. He curled up sideways on the steps and lay there until he thought the night must have passed. Now that it was day, he told himself, someone would come looking for him.

But only Flint and Matt knew where he was. And wasn't Matt at Dorn Hall, wearing Marco's clothes, talking in

Marco's voice? So who would come looking for him? Who would *ever* come looking?

Yet when he heard footsteps above, he began to hope that someone had found him—someone had come to set him free!

The trapdoor swung back. Daylight filled the cellar.

But the voice that spoke was Flint's. "Come on out."

The light hurt Marco's eyes. He felt his way up into the room above. Flint was there alone. He had brought a bottle and something wrapped in a newspaper.

Marco looked toward the door.

"You wouldn't be thinking of going, would you?" asked Flint. "Of course, you wouldn't. You're glad to see me because I've brought you something. I've brought you bread and water and a piece of beef for your dinner."

Marco swallowed. He suddenly knew how hungry and thirsty he was.

"And before I give you all these good things," said Flint, "you're going to do something for me. You're going to tell me what I want to know."

Marco waited.

"There's a big picture in the library at Dorn Hall," said Flint. "You know the one I mean."

"Yes," said Marco.

"There's something behind that picture. Do you know what it is?"

"A safe," answered Marco.

"Quite right. I should have asked you sooner. It would have saved me the trouble of finding it. There *is* a safe behind the picture, and—"

"A safe with nothing in it," said Marco.

"Right again. A safe with nothing in it. That brings up the next question.

Where does your grandfather keep his money?"

"In the bank," said Marco.

"Then what is the safe for?"

"He used to keep things in it. Then a chimney caught fire. We put it out, but after that he said it was foolish to keep money and papers in the house where they might burn."

"So he keeps them in the bank now."

"Yes, he does."

"Are you lying to me?"

"No."

Flint was searching Marco's face. "No, I don't believe you are. I think you know better than to lie to me."

Marco asked, "Why are you keeping me here? What are you going to do with me?"

"It could be the one thing, or it could be the other. Here." Flint handed him the bottle and the bundle wrapped in newspaper. "Back we go now."

Marco went back down the steps. Damp and dark though the cellar was, he was almost glad to be there out of Flint's sight and reach. Something in the man's face frightened him as he had never been frightened before.

CHAPTER TEN

A Visitor

MARCO SAT in the darkness. He held the bottle in one hand and the bundle of food in the other.

The picture was growing clear. Flint had made friends with Varley in the tavern. He had followed him that night. He had beaten Varley so that the old man could never work again. It *must* have been Flint, because he had been ready and willing to take the gardener's place.

All the time he had meant to rob Dorn Hall. There was little money in the house, but there were Grandmother's jewels. There were such things as silver candlesticks and teapots.

With the help of Matt, he would have them all.

Matt. . . . Where had he been for so many years? Why had he come here now to join with Flint against him?

After they robbed Dorn Hall, would Matt and Flint disappear? If they left him here, who would find him?

He felt the bottle in his hand. He could use it to beat on the cellar floor. At the same time he could shout for help. But would anyone be close enough to hear him?

His throat was dry. He opened the bottle and drank a little water. He tore open the bundle and found bread and meat inside. He ate a mouthful. Almost at once he felt sick.

He put the food and water down on the steps. He closed his eyes. After a while he slept.

He woke without knowing how

much time had passed. It might have been hours or days. His arms and legs felt stiff. He stood up and walked about the cellar. It was smaller than he had thought, and once he bumped his head on the wall.

Sounds came from overhead. He listened.

The trapdoor was opening. He looked up into the light. A face looked down—his brother's face.

"I have to talk to you," said Matt. "No—you stay there."

But Marco went up the stairs. Matt was alone. He looked fresh and clean in clothes Marco had once worn.

"Don't come any closer," Matt warned him. "Sit down there. What's the matter with you? Are you hurt?"

"No," said Marco.

"Then why do you walk that way?"

"My legs . . . I've been sitting so long . . ."

"You're pretending, aren't you? You're trying to fool me because you think you can get away. Look." Matt held up a knife with a slim, bright blade. "I've got this, and I can use it. Besides, you can't get past me, because I'm stronger than you." He put the knife into his belt. "Don't come any closer. Sit down!"

Marco sat on one of the wooden boxes.

Matt said in a strange, hoarse voice, "That picture in the library—that's my mother . . . isn't it?"

"It's our mother," said Marco.

"What happened to her?"

"She died."

"I know," said Matt, "but before that?"

"She and I were together in the north country," Marco told him. "Grandfather and Grandmother came for me, but she was dead. They brought me back." Marco asked, "What happened to our father?"

"He died, too."

"Do you remember him?"

"No."

"I remember our mother—a little. I remember you a little, too. We played together. I never knew where you'd gone."

"And you didn't care, as long as you got everything for yourself. Would you really like to know where I went? Would you like to know what happened? I can tell you." Matt's face had grown sharper and older. "Our mother and father were poor and they fought all the time. One day they divided what they had and left each other. They divided us, too. She took one baby, and he took the other. My father was killed in a street fight, and Uncle Flint kept me, when he could. When he couldn't, I had to shift for myself."

"Why didn't you come to me?"

"How was I to know about you? Even Flint didn't know. Oh, he knew you'd been born, but he'd lost all track of you. Then he saw something in a paper about Dorn Hall. He thought some of my mother's people might be there and it might pay him to make them a visit. So he came here. He saw you in the village, and you looked so much like me he thought he was seeing a ghost—"

"Why didn't he tell me who he was?" asked Marco. "Why didn't he tell me about you?"

"What he wanted was money, and he'd never have got any by asking. You and the old people—you'd have fought us, and we wouldn't have got a penny. The rich always win out over the poor. The rich aren't giving up anything. You have to *take* it—"

"No!" said Marco. "I'd have—"

There were steps outside. The door burst open, and Flint was there. His face was pale. His eyes were staring.

"Sneakthief!" he shouted at Matt. "You stole the key. I knew you'd come here. Coming to plot behind my back!"

"I wanted to ask him something, that's all!" cried Matt. "I just wanted—"

Flint raised his fist. Matt leaped out of the way. With one hand, Flint swept Marco through the opening in the floor, and Marco went tumbling down the steps.

CHAPTER ELEVEN

Day into Night

MARCO LAY on the stone floor. The outside door closed, and the house was still.

His brother was gone—he was gone again!

If they could have talked longer he might have made Matt understand. He could have said, "I'll share everything with you. It's what I *want* to do. Let me out, and you'll see."

But Flint had come between them. Flint was always there . . .

Slowly it came to him that something about his prison had changed. The darkness was not so deep. He looked up and saw tiny gleams of daylight along the edges of the trapdoor.

It might mean nothing. Or it might mean that the door was not quite closed.

He climbed the steps and pushed at the door. It moved. Flint had forgotten to slide the bolt in place!

He raised the trapdoor. Up in the room he tried the outside door. It was locked. He kicked it and threw himself against it. The door and the lock held fast.

He tried the window. He knocked out the glass with the water bottle. He pushed and pulled at the bars until he was out of breath, but he could not move them.

So the house was still a prison. But here in the room above the cellar he had light. He had clean air to breathe. Here he could hope and plan again.

He stood on a box and looked out the window. Before him was the beach with low waves breaking on the rocks. If a fishing boat landed, if anyone walked along the shore, he could call for help.

All the rest of the day he watched and waited. Even after night came, he stood watching through the bars. The moon rose over the cliffs. It was a full moon, pale as silver. In its light the sea and shore looked almost as bright as day.

He left the window at last. No fishing boats would be out so late. No one would be walking along the beach.

But he had other thoughts. Sometime Flint might come back, and Marco might surprise him at the door. One blow with the water bottle, one good, swift blow . . .

He ate more of the bread and meat Flint had brought. He was taking a swallow of water when something crashed against the door.

He dropped the bottle. It broke at his feet. The crash came again.

He ran to the window and looked out. Someone was at the door. Someone was smashing at the lock with a stone. It was Matt.

The stone fell from his hand. He was sobbing.

"Matt!" called Marco.

Matt started backward.

"I'm here," said Marco. "I got out of the cellar. Matt, help me."

"I'm *trying*. I've got to get you out!" Matt picked up the stone. "I couldn't get the key again. I thought I could break the lock—" He struck again with the stone. "It won't break—"

"Pry off one of these bars," said Marco.

"How?"

"There's wood." Marco pointed. "Find a piece."

Matt ran down to the shore. In a little while he was back. "There's nothing the right size. And I've got to get you out—" He said something more. His voice broke.

"What?" asked Marco.

"Flint—I think he means to kill you," said Matt, "and he'll kill me if he knows I'm here. Marco, he wants more and more, and there's no stopping him. At first we were going to take the money and anything else we could carry, and that was all. Now he wants me to stay and keep on pretending to be you. If you never turn up, I'll have it all, he says, and he and I can go on living there. He says Grandfather and Grandmother are old and won't be around much longer, and then he and I can have everything."

"Why didn't you go to Grandfather

and Grandmother? Why didn't you tell them?"

"I was afraid. He was always watching. I was afraid for *them*."

"Go to one of the farms. Get someone to help."

"There isn't time. When he finds out I'm gone, he'll know where I went. Marco, he's on his way here now."

"Try the lock again. No, wait. Can you get on the roof?"

"I don't know."

"Bring one of those boards. Put it against the house and climb up."

"Why?"

"The roof is slate. You can break it with a rock."

Matt was off to the pile of boards. He dragged one up to the house. He found a heavy stone and tossed it onto the roof.

Marco heard him climb up and begin hammering with the stone. The slate

was cracking. Pieces of it fell down into the room.

An opening showed over Marco's head. It grew larger. He could see the sky through it.

He set one wooden box on the other and climbed on top of them. He reached up, as Matt reached down and caught his arms.

Matt dragged him through the opening. They slid down the roof and jumped off.

CHAPTER TWELVE

The Cliff

THE BREAK in the cliff was a black, crooked shadow. Marco and Matt headed toward it.

They were nearly there when Matt stopped.

"He's up there!" he whispered.

Marco listened. "Are you sure?"

"Yes," said Matt.

They ran back across the beach.

"We'll hide," said Marco.

"Where?"

Marco turned toward the two houses at the far end of the beach. "There's a place."

"He'd find us there. He'd find us

anywhere on this beach. He's watching us now."

"He couldn't be."

"He is. I know. It's so bright down here. Up there in the path he can look down. Is there another way out?"

"The old road, but—"

"Where?"

"There."

Matt was off. Marco followed him. They took the old road. It wound around the side of the cliff.

"Where does it go?" asked Matt.

"To the top," said Marco.

Matt stumbled over a heap of rocks in the road. "What's that?"

"Slides come down," said Marco.

They ran on.

Marco said, "Careful!"

"What?"

"Don't go so close to the edge."

Matt ran faster. Marco's heart was pounding. "Stop a minute," he said.

"We don't *dare* stop. You don't know—"

Then Matt did stop. Just ahead a slide blocked the way. This was no small heap of stones and dirt. It was as if the road had ended.

Matt turned on Marco. "You said it went to the top!"

"I didn't know about *this*," said Marco.

Matt kicked and poked at the slide. Marco pulled him back. "Don't. You might make a worse one."

They looked over the edge. Far below waves were breaking in a white line against the cliff. The sight left Marco dizzy.

Matt said, "We can't go *that* way."

"We'll have to go down again," said Marco.

Matt stood still. "We can't. Do you hear—?"

Marco heard. From below came the

sound of footsteps. They were neither fast nor slow, and they were steady, as if nothing could ever stop them.

Matt moved to stand in front of Marco. They waited.

And Flint was there. His hair was wild. He was smiling.

"You waited for me," he said. "How very kind of you."

Matt had taken the knife out of his belt. He held it up so that the light shone on the blade.

Flint leaned against the cliff. "You might be more grateful, after all I've done for you. What's happened between us? You're not afraid of me, are you?"

"No," said Matt, but the knife trembled in his hand.

"Here I was hoping we had a plan worked out. I was going to make sure you got what was yours, and you want to throw it all away. It hurts me to see

you like this." Suddenly, in a move too swift for Marco to follow, Flint stooped and snatched a stone off the ground. In the same motion he threw it at Matt's head. He missed.

He looked about him, his eyes darting. There were no more stones at his feet, but there was one in the cliff beside him. He clawed at it. As it came free, a shower of earth and rocks began to fall. From above his head a slide came down. He dropped to his knees. The slide caught him and carried him over the edge of the road. They heard him cry out once as he fell.

CHAPTER THIRTEEN

The Road Back

THE NIGHT was still again. Matt looked at the knife in his hand as if he were surprised to see it there. Slowly he put it away.

Marco was at the edge of the cliff, looking over. He began to shudder.

"Stop it," said Matt.

"I can't," said Marco.

"Let's get out of here."

"We're between two slides."

"This isn't such a big slide. We can dig through it."

"If we dig, more rocks might come down."

"Then we'll go over it. I see a way."

"Come back—" began Marco, but

Matt was already climbing over the heap of rocks and soft earth.

"Come on," he called back.

Marco moved in Matt's tracks. Carefully he made his way over the slide, and he and Matt were safe on the other side.

They started down the road. They hardly spoke until they were on the beach.

Marco looked back toward the foot of the cliff. "Is there any chance he might be—?"

Matt shook his head. "No chance at all."

They crossed the beach. They went up through the break in the cliff and came out at the top.

They rested for a few minutes. The moon was going down.

"Let's go on," said Marco, "while we have the light."

"Go on where?" asked Matt.

"Home," said Marco.

"It's your home, not mine," said Matt.

"It's yours, too."

"After what I've done?"

"You came and helped me get away," said Marco. "If it hadn't been for you—"

"If it hadn't been for me, you wouldn't have been there. None of this would have happened."

"But we're together now. We'll always stay together."

"No!" said Matt. "Not after what I tried to do."

"It wasn't you. It was Flint."

"I can't hide behind Flint. I knew what I was doing. And then those two old people . . ." Matt drew a long breath. "They were good to me. I know they thought I was you. They never knew the difference. But they were kind, and I saw how it could be. . . .

And the picture in the library—it *looked* at me, and—and—I couldn't stand it. I couldn't stand being the way I was."

"Let's go home," Marco said. "To-morrow you can talk to Grandmother and Grandfather."

"I couldn't tell them. And don't you tell them. Not ever."

"They'll have to know," said Marco.

"Why will they?"

"They'll have to know—about Flint. When he doesn't come back—when somebody finds him—then they'll have to know."

"You can tell them this:" said Matt, after a moment. "Tell them you and Flint took a walk to the beach—and he wanted to go up on the cliff road—and he fell. They'll believe you, and it's true, in a way. You tell them that, and I'll go on."

"Where?"

"Somewhere. I don't know yet."

"You can't go."

"I have to," said Matt. "I don't belong here. You don't know about me. I've been things you couldn't ever be. I've been a thief—"

"You won't be again."

Matt looked quietly at Marco. "No," he said. "I won't be again."

"And you'll come back with me."

"I can't."

"Then I'll go with you!"

Matt clenched his fists. "You *fool*—*!*" He stopped, and when he spoke again his voice was gentle. "Let me go. I have to change some things, and when I've changed them, I'll come back. I'll have a *right* to come back."

"You're only saying that, so I'll—"

"I *will* come back."

"You promise?"

"I promise. I swear. Now. Change clothes with me."

They changed clothes.

They walked to where the road began. They shook hands.

Marco took the road. Matt walked off across the field. Marco watched him out of sight, then he turned toward home. The moon had set, but the stars were out, and he could see his way.